igloobooks

Written by Xanna Chown
Illustrated by Sarah Conner, Jacqueline East,
and Lauren Mendez

Cover designed by Nicholas Gage
Interiors designed by Justine Ablett

Edited by Stephanie Moss

Copyright © 2017 Igloo Books Ltd

Published in 2020
by Igloo Books Ltd, Cottage Farm
Sywell, NN6 0BJ
All rights reserved, including the right of reproduction
in whole or in part in any form.

Manufactured in China. 0520 002
10 9 8 7 6 5 4 3

Library of Congress Cataloging-in-Publication
Data is available upon request.

ISBN 978-1-4998-8037-3
IglooBooks.com
bonnierbooks.co.uk

My First
Treasury of
Bedtime
Stories

igloobooks

Contents

Forgetful Fraser

Fraser Fox was very forgetful. One evening, when he was building a super tall brick tower, a cool dinosaur cartoon came on TV.

"ROAR!"

said Fraser.

"Oh dear, Fraser," said Dad. "You forgot to build your tower. Put away your toys and I'll make you a warm drink."

So, Fraser started packing up his wind-up cars and his teddy bears. He stopped when he spotted his rocket ship.

Fraser **zoomed** all around the room, like an astronaut in outer space.

WHOOSH! "Oh dear, Fraser," said Dad, coming back with some warm milk.

"You forgot to clean up. Drink your milk and I'll run you a bubble bath."

8

Dad went upstairs, but instead of drinking his milk, Fraser put the bricks from
his tower back into the toy box. **"I know,"** he thought. **"I'll do it in order."**
So, he put away the red bricks, then the blue ones, then the green ones.

"**Oh dear, Fraser,**" sighed Dad, coming back downstairs. "**You forgot to drink your milk.**" Just then, the doorbell rang and Dad went to answer it. Suddenly, Fraser heard a funny noise coming from the bathroom. "**What's that?**" he thought.

Fraser dashed upstairs to investigate the **splishy, splashy** sound.
"Yikes!" he yelled, when he saw what was happening. The faucet was on
and the bathtub was so full of water that it was about to overflow.

Dad shut the front door, then he heard Fraser **yelp.** He rushed upstairs. Fraser turned off the faucet and stopped the water just in time. **"Oh dear, Dad,"** said Fraser, with a grin. **"You forgot about the bath."**

"I guess you're not the only one who forgets things," said Dad. He chuckled, as his cheeks turned red with embarrassment. "Thank goodness you went upstairs to check. You really saved the day!"

Fraser felt proud. He wouldn't forget about anything again for a while!

Owl Stays Up Late

The sun was rising and it was time for Oscar Owl to go to bed after a busy night. As he flew home, he watched the other animals getting ready for the Big Forest Parade that afternoon. **"I wish I could join in,"** he thought, as they put the finishing touches to their parade floats.

The squirrel twins were decorating their float with pretty leaves, flowers, and lots of glitter and paint, but more of it was ending up on them than on their float! **"We probably won't win a prize,"** giggled the twins. **"But we've had so much fun."**

Even though he was feeling sleepy, Oscar decided to try and stay up so that he could see the start of the parade. **"I know,"** he thought. **"Flying practice will help keep me awake."** So, Oscar **soared** into the sky, trying out new **tricks**, **twirls**, and **loop-the-loops**. **"Woo-hoo!"** he cried.

It wasn't long before Oscar felt so exhausted that his wings wouldn't flap any longer. He glided over the stream and **splashed** his feathers and feet in the sparkly water to wake himself up, but it only made poor, tired Oscar feel cold and wet.

"Maybe a snack will wake me up," thought Oscar, **munching** on some crunchy acorns. He perched in a tree, but soon, his eyes started to feel heavy. He was too tired to notice that the tree was decorated just like the squirrel twins' float for the Big Forest Parade!

Suddenly, the parade float started to move, but Oscar didn't even stir. The parade made its way past the **cheering** crowds, where Magnus Mouse was waiting to judge all the entries. He was amazed to see such a realistic owl on the squirrels' messy float.

"Your float is a bit . . . untidy," said Magnus. "But your owl is so lifelike. I swear I can hear it snoring!"

Then, he awarded the squirrels a special prize. They both felt puzzled. They were sure they hadn't made an owl! Then, they saw Oscar, snoozing in the branches.

"Thank you, Oscar," the twins whispered,
but Oscar just opened one eye and yawned.
"What a lovely dream," mumbled the tired little owl.
He fell straight back to sleep for the whole day, and
never tried to stay up past his bedtime again.

Kit's Tree House

Kit the koala couldn't wait to explore his new tree house. It had big windows, a cool lookout post, and even a tire swing. He was just about to climb the ladder when his sister, Kimmy, pushed past. **"Me first!"** she shouted.

Kit carefully tucked his special blanket into his pocket and climbed after his big sister. **"Don't bring your silly blanket,"** she said bossily. Kit pretended not to hear her. He always took his blanket with him wherever he went.

23

"Let's play superheroes," suggested Kimmy.
"The tree house can be our top secret base!"
"Okay," said Kit happily. He got out his blanket,
ready to play, but Kimmy made a face.
"I don't want to play with that old thing,"
she groaned. "Blankets are for babies!"

SWISH,
WHOOSH!

Kimmy and Kit took turns swinging backwards and forwards on the tire swing.
"Wahoo!" cried Kit, pretending to fly. He wore his blanket like a real
superhero cape and Kimmy couldn't help wishing she had one to wear, too.

25

After lunch, the koalas played space explorers and Kimmy steered the tree house as if it was a spaceship. **BEEP-CLICK-ZOOM!** Then, she giggled when Kit turned his blanket into a puppet and pretended it was a funny little alien, knocking at the window, saying hello!

"Pirates next! The tree house can be our ship," said Kimmy.
To Kit's surprise, she paused and said, "Um . . . maybe your blanket
can be the flag?" Kit felt really pleased. He and Kimmy buried treasure
and battled sea monsters together all afternoon.

27

That night, Kit couldn't wait to fall asleep after a long day of tree house adventures with Kimmy. He clambered into bed and closed his eyes, but something was missing. Suddenly, he realized what it was. **"Where's my blanket?"** he wailed.

Kit jumped out of bed straight away and started searching the house. He looked everywhere he could think of, but the blanket was nowhere to be found. Then, Kit had an idea. **"I know where it is,"** he thought, smiling to himself.

Kit scampered over to the tree house and **scrambled** up the ladder.
He peered inside and, sure enough, fast asleep on the tree house floor was an
exhausted Kimmy, cuddling Kit's special blanket. She'd been too tired after
their day of fun to even make it to bed!

Kit didn't want to wake his big sister, so he snuggled up under the blanket with her and gave her a big, bedtime hug. Then, they fell fast asleep together. After all, just like the tree house, his blanket was special enough to share.

As soon as she heard the alarm clock, Sophie Squirrel **jumped** out of bed. The day of the royal visit was finally here and she couldn't wait to see Princess Hazel in her gleaming coach.

Sophie and her friends had planned to wear their best princess dresses and meet by the old oak tree to wave at the procession. Sophie put on her prettiest dress and tiara, and hunted around for her necklace.

"Oh, Sophie, you look beautiful," cried Mom, as Sophie came into the kitchen. "But why aren't you wearing your new glasses?"

"I can't wear them today," said Sophie.

"Princesses don't wear glasses."

"I'm sorry, Sophie, but you have to wear them," said Mom.

"Besides, I thought you liked them?" Sophie had liked them a lot when she chose them at the glasses shop last week, but today she was going to see a princess. Sophie sighed and went back to her bedroom to put them on.

35

Finally, Princess Hazel rode past, waving royally from her golden carriage. **"Sophie, look!"** cried Betsy. **"She . . . she's wearing glasses, just like yours."**

Sophie couldn't believe her eyes.
"You look exactly like a real princess, now," said Mom.
"I want glasses too!" cried Amelia.
"Can I try them on?" asked Betsy.
Sophie felt so proud. **"Princesses do wear glasses,"** she thought.

That night, Sophie fell asleep still wearing her glasses, and she dreamed very royal dreams.

Baby Toby

Tilly the tiger had a baby brother who was very, very small. He was too small to walk or talk, but there was one thing he could do extremely well . . .

. . . Toby cried so **loudly** that everyone in the house could hear him!

40

One night, Tilly had just drifted off to sleep in her comfy bed, when she heard a noise. **Wah! Wah! Wah!** It was Toby, of course. Tilly **stumbled** sleepily out of bed to see what was going on.

41

Mommy was trying to give Toby a bottle of milk, but he kept pushing it away. "Oh dear," she said, when she saw Tilly. "Did we wake you? I think Toby's growing a new tooth. That always makes babies grumpy."

Tilly went back to bed and pulled the cozy covers up around her ears.

She had just fallen back to sleep, when she heard the noise again.

With a sigh, she got up and peeped sleepily into Toby's room.

She saw Daddy rocking the baby in his arms and singing him a gentle lullaby, but Toby was still **wailing**. "He doesn't want milk and he doesn't want a cuddle," said Tilly, frowning. "What DOES he want?"

44

"I don't know," said Daddy, "but you were just like this when you had a new tooth growing!"

"Was I?" asked Tilly, surprised. She didn't remember being a baby, but she did know what made her feel better whenever she was upset.

Tilly raced to her room and grabbed Pink Monkey from her pillow.
Pink Monkey was a bit tatty from so many years of cuddling, but as
soon as Toby saw his **smiley** face and **cuddly** fur, he stopped sobbing.

46

Toby laid down, sucking Pink Monkey's ear, and within seconds, he was sound asleep. **"Well done, Tilly,"** whispered Daddy proudly, kissing her on the nose. That night, everybody got a good night's sleep, and it was all thanks to Tilly.

Mom switched on Heather's butterfly night-light and promised to stay until she fell asleep. In no time at all, the little hedgehog was dreaming again. This time, her bed grew feathery wings and carried her into the starry sky.

The clouds looked as soft as **fluffy** pillows and, before she knew it, Heather was **bouncing** up and down on them.

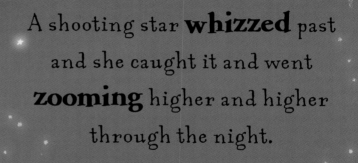

A shooting star **whizzed** past and she caught it and went **zooming** higher and higher through the night.

The star landed in a field full of giant butterflies, whose **dazzling** wings **sparkled** in the starlight. Heather danced with them, feeling as light as a feather, while she **swirled** and **twirled** in the breeze from their wings. Then, a hot-air balloon floated by.

Heather tumbled into the basket, landing beside
a sleepy baby dragon. It was so cute, she couldn't
help stroking its **shimmering** scales.
Suddenly, she heard a strange noise.
Was the tiny dragon **snoring?**

No, it was the sound of Mom pulling back the curtains. Heather opened her eyes, and saw she was back in her bedroom. **"I dreamed about dragons and balloons,"** she gasped. **"But this time they weren't scary at all."**

"That's great," said Mom, smiling. "I knew there was a good dream waiting for you."

"It wasn't just good, it was AMAZING," said Heather. "I can't wait to go to sleep tonight so that I can have another!"

Time for Bed

It was bedtime, but Pip Panda was wide awake.

"Can I have one more story?" he begged Dad. "Pleeeeease?"

Dad laughed. "Okay, Pip," he said. "Just one more."

He opened the Bedtime Treasury book and started to read.

Pip enjoyed the story, but he still wasn't sleepy. **"Your night-lights will help you feel cozy and dozy,"** said Dad. He switched on the **twinkly** lights above Pip's bed and said good night.

Dad was just settling down in his armchair, when he heard a noise coming from the kitchen. He found Pip filling up his cup with water from the fridge. **"I'm a little bit thirsty,"** explained Pip.

Dad tucked Pip back into bed again, but he hopped out.
"I left my blanket in the kitchen," Pip explained.
"I'll get it," said Dad. When he returned, Pip was
rummaging through the wardrobe.

No Such Thing As Monsters

Milo Mouse was very excited to be having his first ever sleepover with his cousin, Tulip. Auntie Jenny tucked him up in a soft sleeping bag next to Tulip's bed and turned off the light. **"Sweet dreams, little mice,"** she whispered.

Milo tried to go to sleep, but there was a strange **gurgling** noise coming from the hallway. It sounded just like a monster's tummy **rumbling!** "Are there any monsters in your house, Tulip?" he asked. "Of course not," said Tulip with a little giggle.

The two little mice crept out of bed and followed the smell downstairs to the kitchen. They saw Milo's uncle cleaning the fridge. **"Oh dear,"** he muttered to himself. **"This old cabbage soup smells terrible."** Relieved, the little mice **scurried** away quietly.

Then, halfway up the stairs, Milo saw a
shadow with pointy claws. **"Help!"** he whispered.
"What is it this time?" sighed Tulip, turning the light on.
"Nothing," giggled Milo, now he could see it was only a coat.

The mice got back into bed again, feeling very sleepy. Tulip had nearly drifted off when she heard a strange noise. It sounded like a monster, **growling** and **snorting** quietly, and it was coming from her bedroom floor!

Click! Tulip turned on the light and saw . . . Milo, fast asleep and **snoring.** "Of course! There's no such thing as monsters," giggled Tulip, but she decided to leave the bedside light on tonight . . . Just in case!

71

Dad asked the girls to collect wood for the fire, so they **dashed** off into
the trees, picking up twigs and **dragging** branches back to the tent.
"Good work," said Dad. "Now you can go and play."

First, they **raced** to the rope swing and took turns **soaring** through the air.

Then, they found a stream and got soaking wet as they paddled in it, slopping **gloopy** mud into a pile to make a tiny waterfall.

After their picnic lunch, Dad organized a sports challenge. Mom cheered when Chrissie came first in the running race.

Mia was the best at tree-climbing and Erin's long trunk helped her win the water fight.
SPLISH-SPLASH!

Mom hung their wet clothes up to dry and the girls changed into their pj's, ready for a delicious supper of sausages and beans. While they ate, Dad told **spooky** stories, which made them **scream** and **giggle**.

As it got dark, the girls snuggled up next
to each other beside the campfire, in their warm
sleeping bags. **"I'm tired,"** sighed Mia.
"Me too," said Erin, yawning.
"Me three," said Chrissie. **"Can we have our
midnight feast tomorrow, instead?"**

"Of course!" said Mom.
"The fresh air and exercise
must have tired you out."
"How about just one marshmallow
before bed?" asked Dad, but the girls
were already asleep, so he popped one
into his mouth. "Ah well, there's
always tomorrow."

The Enormous Teddy

Harley Hippo loved teddy bears. She had so many of them **squashed** into her bed that it was quite a squeeze to fit in herself! "Oh, Harley," said Mom, one morning. **"There's no more room in your bed for any more teddies."**

Harley sat up and all the teddy bears around her **tumbled** onto the floor. **"But we're going to the toyshop today!"** she squealed. **"Can't I make room for just one more?"** Grandma had given Harley some birthday money and she was desperate to add to her collection.

81

Mom smiled. "I'm going to clear out the attic this morning," she said. "If you clean up your teddies and make some space on your bed, then we can go to the toyshop and buy anything you want with Grandma's birthday money."

So, Mom set to work, busily carrying things down from the attic, while Harley took the bears off her bed and put them away neatly.

By lunchtime, Mom had a whole box of things to give away, and Harley had cleared enough space on her bed that she could even see her pillow again!

As soon as they arrived at the toyshop, Harley saw an enormous teddy bear in the window. It was pink and fluffy and was bigger than all the other toys in the shop. It was even bigger than Harley. **"I want that one!"** said Harley, **dragging** Mom inside.

JUNGLETOWN TOYSHOP

It was very difficult to fit Harley AND her new teddy in bed that night, and no sooner had Mom left the room, than she heard a loud

THUMP!

"I fell out of bed!" sobbed Harley.

"**That bear is too big for your bed,**" said Mom, tucking in Harley again, "**but I know where it can sleep.**" She fetched the box of junk she'd cleared out of the attic and pulled out an old hammock.

Mom hung up the hammock and sat the enormous teddy bear inside. **"Perfect,"** she said. **"Thanks, Mom,"** said Harley. Then, she did something she hadn't done for a long time. She stretched out in her bed as wide as she could and fell fast asleep!

Roxy's Rhyme

Mom had been at Grandma's all weekend, so Roxy Raccoon was going to make her a special supper. **"We need a few things from Mrs. Owl's shop,"** said Dad. **"A bag of pasta, a can of peas, two tomatoes, and grated cheese,"** he read from his grocery list.

Roxy giggled. **"It rhymes!"** she cried, as she sang the words back to him. **"I don't need a list at all. If I remember the rhyme, I can tell Mrs. Owl everything we need, all by myself."**

89

"**Okay,**" laughed Dad, as they set off, leaving the list behind. "**When we get there, I'll wait outside.**" Roxy chanted the rhyme over and over again to make sure she wouldn't forget it.

Squirrel Cottage

Roxy **sang** it to a spider, **blurted** it to some butterflies, and **told** it to a toad.

MRS. OWL'S SHOP

Then, Dad asked for something else. "We need flour, too, please," he said. "Then we can bake cupcakes!"
Roxy felt worried. Flour wasn't in her rhyme!

Roxy **dashed** up to Mrs. Owl and repeated the list as quickly as she could before she forgot anything. **"Baggy pasta, tiny peas, tutu tomatoes, great big cheese!"** sang Roxy, getting muddled. **"Oh . . . and one more thing. Can I have some flowers, please?"** she asked.

MILK

BREAD

APPLES

Mrs. Owl looked very puzzled. "Here are your flowers," she said, handing Roxy a bunch of daffodils. "But I'm not sure about everything else. I'll just have to see what I can do."

BLACKBERRY

STRAWBERRY

RASPBERRY

93

Mrs. Owl searched the shelves. "How about . . . a bag of homemade pasta and a can of normal-sized peas, instead?" she suggested.

"These tomatoes don't wear tutus, but they're very tasty. And I do have a big packet of grated cheese."

Dad was impressed that Roxy had bought all the right ingredients for supper and he smiled when he saw the daffodils. **"They won't help us bake cupcakes, but Mom will love them,"** he said.

MRS. OWL'S SHOP

Mom really liked her special dinner, but she loved the flowers even more.
She tucked Roxy up in bed that night, and as Roxy smiled and fell asleep,
Mom whispered, **"It's good to be home."**